Songs of a Certain Humanity

A collection of poetry, lyrics and poetic fables

Robert Spencer Knotts

Songs of a Certain Humanity

Copyright © 2022 by Robert Spencer Knotts

Formatting: Wild Seas Formatting
(http://www.WildSeasFormatting.com)

Cover design: Molly Seabrook

First edition: 2022

Library of Congress Control Number:
2022913916

ISBN:
paperback: 978-1-7339127-2-3
e-book: 978-1-7339127-3-0

Socrates, Emerson & Co.
604 NE 2nd Street, Suite 331
Dania Beach, FL 33004

Contents

LYRICS 55

This book is dedicated to our common humanity,
the core of goodness and inherent value within every person.

"If you want to awaken all of humanity, then awaken all of
yourself.
If you want to eliminate the suffering in the world, then
eliminate all that is dark and negative in yourself. Truly, the
greatest gift you have to give is that of your own self-
transformation."
Lao Tzu

"You must not lose faith in humanity.
Humanity is an ocean;
if a few drops of the ocean are dirty, the ocean does not
become dirty."
Mohandas K. Gandhi

Preface

Reading a new poem for me is first a feeling. I allow the poet's words to roll through me unquestioned, much as I experience an unfamiliar work of music. Though I'm analytical by nature, often too much so, I try to set aside any serious analysis for a time. I ask myself a single question: "What does this poem make me feel?"

But of course any good poem has many layers. That's one trait possessed by poetry over verse – the poem uses language in fresh ways to express much more than it seems to say. Exploring those connotations and references and linguistic connections, the suggestions and implications, makes poetry what it is. Poetry is the highest and richest form of human expression through words.

I began writing poetry sometime in my youth. Well, writing verse in any case. The first "poem" I can recall with certainty was written when I was 16-years-old during my brief romance with ski racing, rhyming stanzas that linked success on the snow with faith in God. I still have the short work somewhere hidden among my many loose papers. You will be glad to hear, no doubt, that I did not include it in this collection.

These poems, lyrics and poetic fables emerged only after long years as a professional writer, starting in 1997 with "Evergreen Memorial." The most recent was "Waiting for the Sky to Burn," which I completed in early 2022. Over those 25 years, my writing matured and my perspectives evolved significantly. In 1995 I founded a federally recognized nonprofit group, the Humanity Project, to promote my profound belief in the value of each human being and in humanity itself – a nonprofit that now offers acclaimed free programs and materials to both children and adults. And in 2019 I published "Beyond Me: Dissecting Ego To Find The Innate Love At Humanity's Core

(A New Psychology As Philosophy)," a 600-page nonfiction work that I researched for decades and wrote over a difficult half-decade. That nonfiction book offers what I firmly believe to be a highly original, greatly detailed explanation of our humanity at the deepest levels: new and verifiable theories of psychology that lead to a most hopeful understanding of where we now are and where we yet may go as a species. Anyone who devotes the energy to reading every page of that book with an open mind and then trying to grasp the real meaning is likely to come away with a fuller, more optimistic view of themselves and others. I think "Beyond Me" is a book that will change those who honestly consider its ideas … a claim I offer without arrogance or ego, believe me.

All this is worth the mention because most of the poems, some of the lyrics and all of the poetic fables emanated from those same ideas. By now, as I close in on age 70, I have written millions of words since my first professional paycheck in 1980. I assembled a good number of those words into 26 books, five plays, countless works of journalism. And 40 poems, 14 lyrics and a dozen fables collected here in my 27th published book. Along with "Beyond Me," these are among my writings I most cherish.

Some required extended labors, others came together in minutes. As an example I began "September 11, 2001" shortly after that terrible attack on the United States, writing much of it in a matter of days. But the final stanza eluded me for months as I tinkered with the other wording already written down in longhand. (That poem is now in the Artists Registry of the National September 11 Memorial & Museum in New York City, by the way. It is the only poem or lyric in this collection that I have published in any meaningful form before now. The fables all appear on the Humanity Project website. And I also recorded an audiobook of the 12 fables, each accompanied by a different piece of music composed and performed by me:

"Fabled Lives.") By contrast with my September 11 poem, I wrote "How Long This Time" in 15 minutes at my computer as an immediate online improvisation for a Facebook post in response to the 2019 back-to-back mass shootings in El Paso and Dayton.

Though I'll let you navigate these pieces for yourself, I do feel some of them benefit from a bit of context. This may prove especially useful in later years, as technology leaves behind a poem such as "Voice Wrecked Mission." I wrote it sometime in 1998, when I'd bought my first computer with built-in voice recognition. In sampling the new application, I began dictating in hopes this might be an easy way for me to write emails. It wasn't, as I quickly discovered – and it still isn't all this time later. Voice recognition-to-print remains primitive at best. But as I dictated a series of phrases to my computer back in '98, I discovered that some words had been transformed entirely by the perplexed software. My machine had misinterpreted some spoken sentences but recorded other words correctly, leaving behind a paragraph of one user's annoyed attempt at poetic dictation. I reworked that random mishmash as a basis for my poem, adding and altering to make the point in what I hoped was a fresh, amusing way.

"Litturari Agence" expresses another source of my frustrations with the writing life. It may ring true to my fellow professional writers. "On Morning Grass" was my first haiku in many years, written during Spring 2022. "Seduced" and both poems entitled "Illness" (parts one and two) reflect my painful personal experiences with various ailments … and my hardwon belief that all physical disease begins and lingers as a result of the forces within our minds. "When The Frobblerocks Came To Tipplytea" is a rhyming children's poem inspired by my lifelong admiration of Dr. Seuss. (I think it would make a fine picture book.) And then there are two poems very different indeed from the others, both written in 2004 – and requiring a few words of explanation: "Fuck" and "Monogamy." Though my views on such matters have modified over the ensuing 18 years, I included these pieces because I like them both. And because they are a sincere outpouring of my feelings at that time, each poem and each title very deliberately provocative. They never were intended to advocate promiscuity, mind you, but rather a more authentic and open approach to sexuality grounded in human necessity. I have always regarded sex as an opportunity for emotional bonding between individuals, even the more casual varieties of sex. I still do. These two poems question the conventional attitude toward sexual relationships, suggesting that the traditional just might require a rethinking in some fashion. (As an aside, I really should mention that I enthusiastically recited both poems at two public spoken word forums soon after finishing the pieces. At the first event, they were applauded loudly. At the second, well, it was a very different crowd. After the most tepid sort of applause, one sympathetic poet near me leaned in and whispered, "Now that's a poem right there!")

Several of my poems attempt to convey something through the briefest possible wordplay, as in "Happy Hour" and "Living." Others explore their subject more thoroughly, including "I Too Dream" and "Requiem for a Journalist." As for the lyrics, all but two inspired my own music to accompany them: I've not yet needed to compose tunes for "More or Less" or "Let's Take a Walk." My fables began with "The Tale of Techie Tom" in 2006, "The Tale of the Two Windows" being the most recently written in 2019.

If I live long enough, I would expect to write more fables, more lyrics and more poems. I'm hopeful. But the diverse works here collected already reveal quite clearly my core beliefs and values. I believe in the human individual. I believe each of us is far too hard on ourself. I believe this inner turmoil causes us no end of personal and social problems. But I also believe, oh yes I know, that humanity very very slowly transcends our misery and our ignorance – "advancing on Chaos and the Dark," as Emerson wrote. And so above all I believe in the ascent of humanity. Perhaps these writings may help you to feel some of that optimism too.

POEMS

I Too Dream

I too dream a world
but unlike worlds most
dreamed before.

Mine is a world
pocked by bickering and war,
snarling people
and barking mobs.
Oh yes, I dream of human beings
foaming yet with angers
and fizzing still with fears
bred by the familiar misunderstandings
among careless flung words.

All beings as themselves
so human,
then as now.

But all with one thing imagined
more for those living
in my vivid world anew.

Because my dreaming dreams of
future skirmish-wars defused,
our old hatreds resolving
in a new confidence of knowledge
that wedges aside the ancients
of myth and superstition
lingering indifferently
from millennia elapsed.
I dream of bicker noises
overtaken by song,
the transcendent hymn
of our humanity
crescendoing in a joyful ode

whenever the voices of dissonance
again rise to a din.

Oh yes, dissonance shall surely sound again
and often again in that world I dream,
disharmony intrinsic to a cosmos atonal,
a natural music playing ever out of key
in the chaos of clash and clatter
written into nature's grand score.
We are organisms
fashioned of conflict.
Crossed purposes of interests and
crosscurrents of histories
will move us then as now,
the panting passions of our peoples
still puffed up and selfish centered.

We cannot be more than we are made.
But we need not be less.

Yes when I dream of human beings
being as the human finally fulfilled,
every member of our envisioned species
then understands that existence without
conflict has always been fantasy,
a conjuring of Utopia unattainable
amid a universe propelled
ever by the myriad colliding
streams of necessity.

Nature's legacy to human beings
is conflict, oh yes,
but conflict resolved by reason
is humanity's gift to nature.

In this world I dream about
judgment will nearly

balance out emotion,
the angers and fears of this moment
dissolving soon in the wisdom
of the next.

We cannot be more than we are made.
But we need not be less.

As an infant develops to a child
who ages to an adult
who may evolve to a
human being wondering and wise,
so humanity still toddles
toward our maturity,
wobbling step by
faltered step in
the long long childhood.

I dream this child standing
one day a young adult
proud and imperfect,
oftentime curious with uncertainty,
straining to discern the confusing paths
forward before advancing
forcefully in bold stride.

A Song For Today

How trite we have become,
how predictable the words,
wrinkled lips expressing
wrinkled imaginations.

When will it happen?
How will it come?
Have you heard –
It's happening now to some …

"Last month they found Sybil's tumor,
Do you know what her doctor said then?"

"Harry's got those tests next week,
And then that surgery who knows when."

"The red pills make me very dizzy,
And I must ask the cardiologist for more."

"Scared myself to death last night
When I fell down hard in the discount store."

Perhaps instead let's look
for time to listen,
just listen, yes,
let us listen just for a time.

Together hear the watersongs and the earthcalls
sounding from the garden as we stroll.
Listen.
We might yet discover
whispered arias of flower leaves
or thrumming plainchants
of pale spring petals.

Yes, let's both listen.
And listen again.
No more about our pill bottles for a while.
Cancel all conversation about
post-procedure complications
and the follow-up prognosis.
Tear up the payment plans
reserving private places
that will offer us
no garden songs,
only silence.

Just smile with me today.
And listen.
Shhhhh …
The music still plays for us
if we only cock our head a bit
to hear with our good ear.

Too Long Lingering

I once wrote a free verse poem in my teens
claiming "lies, constant lies"
plagued this earth.

But now aged well in my sixties I know
that it's wisdom, not truth,
most in dearth.

Those lies just arise from uncurious thoughts,
which emerge with the words
from our past.

We're a species encoiled in cords knotted too tight
by the hands that manhandled
them last.

And so now I read patient poets who see
there must be much wiser
ways

To untie our knots of ignorant truths
that still linger from earliest
days.

Turtle Rain

Did you ever feel you're
like a turtle in the rain?

Though you're made for water,
too much water seems a pain?
Tough enough to take it
and you're all wet anyway.
But some turtles still just
pray for partly sunny days.

Did you ever feel you're
like a turtle in the rain?

Waiting For The Sky To Burn

Now we've arrived one score and two.
A new millennium's no longer new.
Pricked by fever and breathing hard
As shrapnel scatters in our yard.
Our thermostats can't stand the strain
When blizzards fall as blistering rain.

And so we sit and wait our turn,
Looking for the sky to burn.

Surely pessimism's just and fair
With dull pandemic in our air.
Air smudged by coalclouds low and warm
To stir up catastrophic storm.
Drone blitzkrieg adds gunpowder haze
Above the slaughtering field of days.

And so we sit and wait our turn,
Looking for the sky to burn.

Whatever can I hope to do
To swallow facts before I chew?
No one's quite up to the task
To answer things before I ask.
I walk a staircase downward stark
Toward the basement of the dark.

So now I sit and fret my turn,
Waiting for the sky to burn.

I wonder what they must have thought
When decimating plagues were fraught.
Or when their world was hard at war.
Did they foresee endtimes before?
It must have seemed full just and fair

To feel the panic and despair.

I suspect the crowds took turns
Looking for their sky to burn.

Somehow I understand them all
Imagining the deathblow's fall.
That's what imagination does,
Making real what never was
And probably will never be
If we're to judge from history.

Perhaps we've time to make the turn,
Looking yet for what's unlearned:
Apocalypse that disappears
Once we peer closely in the mirror.

A Saving Grace

As if a whistling
of neighbors I follow
home from a forest fog,
come the earliest
birdsongs of night
to guide me,
frightened,
from my bedcovers
toward dawn.

Unfeathered Flights

What must a bird think of a plane?
Does it seem forbidding as a flame?
Or part of the landscape like a cloud?
Or simply annoying and simply too loud?

Or perhaps something envied, something admired.
Something so strong it would never get tired.
Something so fast it could migrate in hours.
Something so colorful it feeds on the flowers.

Just one of their kind,
If quite hard to explain
For a small-bodied bird
With no big bird's big brain.

But how large are its eggs and where do they nest?
How does a plane mate and produce all the rest?
How can it fly without flapping its wings?
Have birds noticed there's only one song each plane sings?
A screech that frightens all others away.
And why don't planes soar the windcurrents for play?

Yes, what must the birds think of our flying machine?
Does a plane seem erotic, heroic or mean?

Or maybe we're arrogant to imagine they worry
about some featherless flier always in such a hurry.

A Poet's Residue

Perhaps it is merely the
accumulated metaphors
that dampen me.

It surely is not the
cafe chattings cancelled
or the wet socks,
not the simple, persistent impracticality
of seven weeks' unyielding rains,
but instead my unquestioned
acceptance of cliche that produces
my inclement moods.

I too have absorbed our
common vocabulary of misery,
the stormy words and rainy phrases
still recited to us tiredly and tirelessly,
entirely independent of any forecast.

Yet if only I remove this poetic residue,
separate the fresh observation
from the stale suggestion,
the crystalline droplets slipping
from the leaves of my
black olive tree now
appear as cheerful as any
intensity of sunshine
radiating optimism.

Happy Hour

Olive olives.

The Hammer and the Nail

It slips me back through centuries
The sound of hammer against nail

Despite nearby contempored noise,
Electrobeep and digiwail.

In the distance I hear carpenter
Assembling one by one

Exactly as the 1845
Youth once had done.

Or the pegnailers of London
Building stages for a bard.

Or the labormen of Boston
Creating Common out of yard.

Today's clap of steelsplit wood
Travels much the same

And delivers me to moments
That suggest what we became.

A Dog's Life

I'm like that dog
in an open-end cage.
I never quite learn
though I'm mangy with age.

Right behind the poor mutt
there's no wall at all,
a clear three-sided box
something like a glass stall.

Still, the starving dog tries
to break through to his food
without pausing to strike
a more reasonable mood.

What he wants is in front
just outside the clean glass
so he bangs the box hard
with his head and his ass.

When all he need do
is walk calmly around
and devour the meal
without making a sound.

How often I feel
such irrational ire
when something I want
fogs my head with desire.

I can't seem to step back
for a clear-eyed perspective
or just glance behind
to become more selective.

What I want, what I need
appears nearly in reach,
so close I forget things
that dog just might teach.

I stare without blinking,
I pant for my prize,
then I barge straight ahead
without shifting my eyes.
And quite like the canine
who's blinded by passion,
I bang and I bash
in my Blind Bob fashion.

Oh, how I so wish
I could just learn to reason
in ways somewhat better
than critters with fleas on.

The Silent Faces

Ah yes,
I know you once dove out an airplane
with your bravery on full display.
And you've clambored up clouded mountains
and frightened the eagles away.

Through the ocean's uncertain deeps
you explored limits real and implied.
Yet I wonder if you can confront
the silent faces you hide.

To sit quiet alone for one hour
and watch as they all appear.
Perhaps the true test of courage
is the one that you find in a mirror.

September 11, 2001

Why?

They shattered our glass sky,
and three thousand human shards
tumbled through holes made in
jetcraft silhouettes.

Did you see them disappear?
Did you ask the question?

Not for Jesus or Abraham this time.
Not for the swastika, the rising sun
or even the crescent moon.
You may not like the answer.
But if you would look,
turn inward.

Find the hovel where all
your secret rage demands explanations.
Find the streetcorner where all
your hidden self-contempt begs for revenge.
Find the cave where all
your private fears grovel for redemption.

Try then, if you can, to imagine
this cacophony of desperation
without respite or reprieve,
listening always to those morning prayers
and evening exhortations,
a permanent dissonance
with all silence, all peace denied,
long denied,
too long denied.

Until now.

Blind Optimism

This turtle's
quite randy I've
noticed that but …

his charms all
seem lost on this
dropped coconut.

An Omni Present

(In Celebration of Jill's Birthday – November 15, 2003)

It is a presence so pervasive
that its presence seems to vanish,
like the ceaseless seawhispers
to a mariner's ears,
murmured in hushes beneath the bow,
noticed never and always
until only silence would sound unsettling.

And so this disquieting permeation of me.

I have searched but found
no word for this feeling.
Not devotion, not lust
and surely not love.
Those only fix the others in memory,
each more easily defined than you.

It is such indefinites as this that frighten sometimes,
and I am frightened sometimes
by something undescribed
among all the wisdoms on passion
I have read explained.

It is such intensities as this that frighten sometimes,
and I am frightened sometimes
by something undescribed
among all the experiences of passion
I have heard recalled.

This presence is many presences in portions,
one feeling made up of parts,
some grateful, anxious appreciation of
my unyielding sexual need for you

and the surprise at my unfaltered
delight in your company,
with laughter.
You,
of profound intelligence and unguarded gentleness
and both generosity and empathy expressed without
expectation.
It is you that I feel.
The awareness comes now only with the pause.

And so it is with the longest sailor,
who sometimes stops after all
for a moment listening at last
to those soft exquisite feminine
suggestions of the sea
speaking perpetually of something
he never fully comprehends.

Dawned Upon

Dawn comes
as a concept,
diffuse indigos
that gather enbrightened
unsurely
until they
at last reveal
one recognition
anew
in compact
roselight array.

Nature's Ways

Some animals must
beat their brains
to forage food
between the rains.

But some find feasts
just hanging there
ripe outside
their treetop lair.

Each knows to
disregard the hype.
Life isn't fair
for any stripe.

Some get less
and some get much
and some make do
with such and such.

But if a fair world's
still your hunch
just watch woodpeckers
eating lunch.

How Long This Time

How soon until we grow weary?
How many hours of online ire?
On what day do we decide it's just useless?
At what point does our outrage tire?

When will we just throw our hands up,
Conceding there's nothing to do?
How long til the news stories fade,
And statistics no longer feel true?

Today each of us cares keenly.
Today the body count's fresh.
But tomorrow the toll becomes memory,
Surely somebody else's mess.

Hidden Colors

(Dedicated to Sondra Knotts Lucas,
my sister, on her 70th birthday)

Sometimes the wait is very long
before the proper moment
at last can come along.

An eventful preparation until a time is finally right.

But when the waiting has disappeared,
after the bud is fully nourished by
the extended summer's night,
then dawnlight will reveal all blossomed
multi-colors that had been hiding here.

Chalk & Cheese

Even chalk and cheese are alike
In some ways.
Two brothers who once roomed
In very early days.

Now separated by distance
And separated by thought.
Separated by feelings
And by wars that we fought.

Mother and Father

Mother

I was molded by
The shape of your
Severe corners
Exaggerated angles
Razored edges.

Father
I was smoothed by
The scrape of your
Rounding curves
Gentling arcs
Softened textures.

Oh, You!

Oh, you inventor of
the leafblower!
Oh, you creators of
the backup beeper
and the car alarm!
I must say,
if you can hear me,
that I'm deaf
to your inventions'
charm.

Propelling vegetation from
here to there
rarely makes much sense,
piling foliage against
my fence.
Outdoor clutter scattered
into an opposing wind
is pointless give and take.
What, then, was wrong with
the broom and the rake?

And as for those warnings
when in reverse,
we might do better
just to rehearse
some simple habits of
careful driving.
Like looking behind
before we move.
Instead those beeps annoy
to prove
the accident victim is to blame,
as companies claim

now without shame.

Then there is that
break-in prevention
to which no one pays
even slight attention.
Beset by constant noises
the people merely
raise their voices
to be heard above
such alarming din,
pulsing blasts ignored
whether from within
Rolls, Hyundai or Ford.

If our ears could speak
instead of listen
what would they say
do you suspect?
Would they complain
of our abuse?
Protest against technology
so ill-used?
Beg for finger-plugs
against the dissonance?
Or just politely dismiss
humans as a nuisance?

Oh, you inventors of these
noise pollutions,
your creations gave us
no solutions
and should be stored
upon some dusty shelf.
Next time please just keep
your ideas to yourself.

Fuck

Fidelio asexualis,
of the unsexual sisterhood
and this brotherhood of monks.
Amen.

From some tonsured fearbearers
perhaps came our fettered precept
of devotion by unfucking,
all the psalms of self-denial
in every language to memorize.

We have endured
and we have allowed the
unfucking of humanity,
constrained first by virulent edict
and now by exhausted belief,
until the limping legions
of semi-sexuals
think of almost nothing else but
"S - -"!!

*Deny thyself
and thou shalt want!*

"We are gathered here today
to join this happy, credulous couple,
who promise they will
never fuck another
and so soon will
never want to fuck
each other either,
til death do them part,
relieved at last."

*Deny thyself
and thou shalt need!*

"Remember always, boys and girls,
this is what we mean by
lovers being true:
Keep those zipper teeth clenched
when you're away from home.
Remember always,
Unfuck you!"

*Deny thyself
and thou shalt take!*
Or simply stop in time
caring,
all caring.

Perhaps it is we, the shackled monolovers,
who must arise at last
each to tell our solitary, frustrated partner
we despise the unfucking
that for centuries has
uncum to be –
and then, yes, joyful and guiltless
unzip now for our
own humanity.

Monogamy

Steak is my very
favorite food,
I have finally decided.
Yum!

So I will never taste
one crumb
of
anything else.

Why risk pork chops?

FaceTwit: 2019

Our modern walks,
from screen to screens.

Tightrope upon
some cyberbeams.

Unbalanced by
thin etherthreads.

A dangerous tread
with dizzyed heads.

Very Often Indeed

Always
is
always
wrong…

With some exceptions

On Morning Grass

I awaken to

the payfulness of squirrels

on the morning grass.

Living

Bring
loved before
to now
for next…

Seducer

No lover is so seductive
as affliction.

We fall in love again at
our new illness's first fluttering glance,
a shy sidelong smile infatuating,
promising all suffering's distractions,
yes, all the romance of our dis-ease.

"Take me away, please,
from all of this!"

But like so
many love affairs
these almost always,
always,
go pretty ugly
in the end.

Illness (part one)

You can turn queasy
with seasickness
on dry land
or suffer the miseries
of Himalayan altitudes
at sea level
if you only believe
wrong

Illness (part two)

Cancer anyone?
Heart attack?
Sciatica?
Back pain?
Eczema?
Seborrhea?
Multiple Sclerosis?
Muscular Dystrophy?
Carpal Tunnel?
Headaches?
Irritable Bowel Syndrome?
AIDS?
Ebola?
Cold?
Flu?
Allergies?
Overweight?
Hypertension?
Alzheimer's?
Diarrhea?
Nausea?
Etc. etc. etc. etc.
Or just nearsightedness?

Voice Wrecked Mission

This is a simple dictation. Sample dictation. I am trying to speak normally, slowly. Unlucky use this for a male. I wood like to use this for my electronic mail. My question is this? I wonder how will it works? It's seems that it maybe difficult. But it seems it will be difficult. It is an interesting technology. But not quite usable yet period. Are out paragraph new field new field Roman no listen roaming all across the land sitting by the wayside by the babbling brooks of York yellow mom's singing brightly York selling and no you are yes you are not York period York so silt and no silly yes silly toy silly toy. This is almost tow a tree. It electronic poetry. Listen to it rights in high into the night sky rambling and ruling and not ruling rolling and rustling like the leaves of winter. Paragraph new field new field no listen new field. When trees seized of electronic be late. So much for the wonder us joys love dictation. Butter wraps it is poetry after all.

Liturrari Agence

All sunglass and smile,
Indoors,
Holding licked fingers
To the same wind.

Some Call It Science

Science is great when it works,
without data collected by jerks.
They issue such firm proclamations
as if testing the limits of patience
with this day's wondrous new potion
and that next day's opposite notion.
One food will help us live long
til new study shows that was wrong.
Miracle pills are prescribed with conviction
before patients report their addiction.

Experiments and numbers and findings
seem useful for truth unwindings
but the truth is we're often misled
by the experts whose truths we are fed.

Please trust me, I do adore science
when real insight is held in reliance.
And yes, I know there's some range
for meaningful truths to change.

But is there any excuse
for facts that are merely a ruse?
Too many in white coats still thrum
with knowledge that simply is dumb.

Requiem For A Journalist

How often I miss the clatter of our typewriters,
wax nostalgic about
the contented, innocent years
of Vietnam
and race riots
and Watergate.
Useful days
of ink and blood.

But now we're told the times demand new fashions,
journalistic styles changing each season with the hemlines.
Chasing documents is unnecessary when we can chase
comments,
passing paparazzi as we run.
Marketing surveys prove our best reports leave out all
bewildering facts.
And we have no need for what was quaintly called news
judgment
when our news judgment pours off the official government
fax.

Editor's Note:
In the interest of accuracy
We will state our position this one time:
We wish neither to offend nor inform.
We'll print anything to make our circulation climb.

"The news is just another business today," the glass offices
insist.
And they point out, without regret,
that the era of Woodstein and Cronkite is gone.
This is the Age of Pizazz.
All Color, All The Time.
Twenty-four hours of quotelets,

online or on cable,
for a population too busy – or maybe too confused – to know.
"The new 3D graphics are hard-hitting," the glass offices
smile.
"With these statistics, we'll sum up the world in a chart."
"Strip that Madonna interview across the top of 1A!"
"Will sources confirm Hillary called Monica a 'young tart?'"

This Just In:
Live from our NewsCam Center tonight
We'll report this one simple truth before we say goodbye:
We wish neither to offend nor inform.
We'll say anything to keep our ratings high.

I can't explain the when of this incident.
And I'll never tell you the why or the how.
The rest of the facts hold no interest.
For some reason, no one is interested in anything now.

At this writing, everything is just allegation.
When this mystery will be solved, time will tell.
We admit that we're dealing only in rumor.
But at least rumor helps newspapers sell.

Maybe it happened after all the corporate mergers.
Maybe it happened after the shearing of the editor's balls.
Maybe it started with the news director's sense of failure.
Or maybe it's just the Oprah in us all.

Before Dawn

Lugubrious falls
first off the edge
this morning,
landing melodiously in
a splatter of ink.

The long lugubrious
lines of language that
eventually stumble
to their knees
and spread wide
their grateful arms
and weep.

2DDG – L, B

Her wordjoys, a softness zephyr
between the storms.

Her smiletouches, a lightness welcome
within the rejections.

Her eyelights, a gentleness acceptance
among the sorrows.

And then
inviting inviting inviting
she takes me,
all loveliness embracing,
into it all.

You, Perhaps

When your heart whispers,
the echo resounds in thought.
"Phony," goes the murmur
and the crescendo of repetitions,
but never followed by a question:
"Is it so?"
For why doubt the received truths of your youth,
all the vast visceral accumulated wisdom of
one brief childhood?

"Fool," you hear softly
and soon enough it is real again
as always before.
The ungentle accusations gently follow one on one,
unchallenged as the faint clicks inside a watch,
as the muffled drumtaps of the breast,
their reverberations sounding loudly
and believed.

And this is all that's needed.
For believing makes it so.

Evergreen Memorial

The rock outlives the flesh,
but not by long.
Before the absence of the great-granddaughters of the great-
granddaughters,
the pitiless white abrasives of the wind and rain
scour away even this stolid remembrance,
wash clean the stone.

A smile vanished.
Then a form.
Then a name.

Only the growing grass to mark the place,
fertilized by bone.
And the scents of fresh wisteria
and wild lime and purple jacaranda
and the recent droppings of a cocker spaniel.
And all the worn gray fragments of the earth,
settled among the cypress and the spanish moss and the shit,
reminders of the passing and the passed.

When The Frobblerocks Came To Tipply Tea

The Frobblerocks came down one day
to the village of Tipply Tea.
They wore their billygoat beards
And coats made from wings of bees.

The Frobblerocks had Mean Tags on their sleeves
and sneers on their Frobblerock faces.
And they talked too loud and pushed through crowds
and made the worst of all the best places.

Before the invasion of the Frobblerocks
the Tipply Teans always sang and danced.
They danced and sang their Tipply Tea tunes
about friendship and sweet romance.

But Frobblerocks had no time to dance and sing
and hated every kind of romance.
Instead they preferred to growl and punch
and put frogs down each other's pants.

And they were strong too!
One Frobblerock was stronger than any Tipply Tea three.
Just a look at a Frobblerock fist proved
Frobblerocks were strong and tough as could be.

What could the Tipply Teans do?
What would you do if this happened to you?

"Fight back!" a few - though only very few -
feisty Tipply Teans said.
But most others argued, "No! Not that!
We'll only win by using our heads!"

So they gathered in little Tipply Tea groups
and strained their Tipply Tea noggins,
while the Frobblerocks yelled and hit and kicked
and built fires with Tipply Tea toboggans.

When the Tipply Teans finally came out of their homes
they had a plan to get rid of their nasty invaders.
A plan so cool and so clever and so crafty
it might have come from Supersmart Spacemen Planmakers.

They talked, the Tipply Teans did.
And that's all they did was talk and talk
about some place out among the forest.
Another town so close that it was just a close walk.

A town called Snooterville, the Tipply Teans said,
where every Snootervillian had much more than their fill
of ice cream and candy and cookies and cakes.
All those sweet things just over that hill.

And the Frobblerocks listened and heard the tales,
over and over, about the Snooterville goodies laying around.
They heard it so much that one Frobblerock finally said,
"Hey, let's go take over that town!"

So some jumped on each other's shoulders
but most just scrambled over their fellow Frobblerocks' backs.
And like a herd of bulls they stampeded toward Snooterville
dragging empty cookie boxes and huge Stolen Candy sacks.

Over the grassy hills the Frobblerocks ran wildly,
pushing and wrestling angrily to reach the sweet foods first.
The Frobblerocks were bad before this Snooterville dash,
but now all their nasty badness just grew worse.

And then suddenly this rotten group was there, but where
was there?
The sign said Snooterville but no candy was anywhere in
sight!
How could this be "there" with no cakes or ice cream around?
And the furious Frobblerocks screamed, "No, it's impossible!
This sign can't be right!"

But the sign was right - This was Snooterville for sure.

And that was the clever part of the Tipply Tea plan.
For every Tipply Tean knew Snooterville was a place
without sugars or spices or even one cake pan.

Instead Snooterville was a town filled with birds of every
kind,
birds of every wonderful flock and every beautiful feather.
And all the birds sang happy songs throughout every day,
in yellow sunshine or in blue rain or in any color weather.

The Tipply Teans knew no one could leave Snooterville after
they entered
and there was no way to silence the lovely bird songs.
Of course only a Frobblerock would want to escape
a land where pretty bird music played all day long.

The Frobblerocks could only hear song after song after song
about friendship and sweet romance.
But not one song ever mentioned growling or punching
or putting frogs down anyone's pants.

And slowly, very slowly at first,
the bird songs began to change the Frobblerocks.
Do you believe these foul Frobblerocks started to smile?
Why, they even put on clean hats and socks.

They stopped their yelling and growling
and they left the Snooterville frogs alone.
And some Frobblerocks began to feel that, just maybe,
Snooterville wasn't such a bad home.

And then, after a time, the Frobblerocks themselves started to
sing songs.
Honestly, they did! Soon they sang day and night.
Songs about friendship and kindness and love.
They were so busy singing they forgot to start fights!

And after quite a while longer,
when only music and love filled every Frobblerock heart,

the Frobblerocks found they were suddenly free to leave
Snooterville.
They could leave in a bus or a train or even an ox cart.

But all of them just danced happily back to Tipply Tea.
And the Frobblerocks asked - this time politely asked - to stay.
So without hesitation the Tipply Teans sang out these words:
"Yes, please do!
We'd love you to stay since you've all changed in this way!"

And to this day, not far from the beautiful Snooterville birds,
just beyond the forest and over that hill,
is the peaceful village of Tipply Tea,
where the Frobblerocks and Tipply Teans live together still.

They sing all their happiness
and they dance all their joy.
And not a single Frobblerock
looks for someone to hurt or annoy.

And if you listen hard
when it's very quiet at night,
you might hear all the Tipply Tea villagers
sing out their love and delight.

But if you can't quite hear those songs
you'll just have to sing one of your own.
Maybe some song you make up
or some song you heard at home.

It's not hard to sing, as the Frobblerocks learned,
If you just smile and sing out you can't ever go wrong.
And perhaps if you smile and sing happily enough
you'll make everyone so happy they will sing right along.

LYRICS

Passing By

As I sit by the sea,
I smell mountain meadows.
When I touch the wet earth,
I feel the blue sky.
As I walk through the field,
I wade the cool river.
And think of the things that are passing us by.

As I sigh at the clouds,
I smile at the raindrops.
When I laugh at the moon,
I soon start to cry.
As I hear winter winds,
I sing summer breezes.
And think of the things that are passing us by.

Why should I talk with the forest?
Why should I dance with the sea?
Why understand that each woman and man
Must dream much the same things as me?

As I see the sun fall,
I feel that it's rising.
Yes, I watch the rose bloom,
Then I open my eyes.
As I look at the stars,
I can't help but wonder
'Bout all of the things that are passing me by.
Yes, all of the things that are passing you by.
All of the things that are passing us by.

Sometimes, But Always You

Sometimes it seems it doesn't pay to get up,
When both sides are the wrong side of the bed.
But the whispers of your smile
Murmur to my heart a while,
And make the wrong side right for me instead.

Sometimes it seems that all the colors have gone,
My day's a faded film in black and white.
But your laughter makes me feel
That you've somehow changed the reel,
This dull, gray movie suddenly looks bright.

Living isn't life
Without you anymore,
It's eating steak
Without a fork and knife.
Funny isn't fun
Without you anymore,
I guess you really are
The only one.

Sometimes I just can't see the up from the down,
My plans look like a blueprint without blue.
But you help me see the scheme,
Find directions for my dream,
And then I'm sure I'll build this dream with you.

Sometimes it seems it doesn't pay to get up,
When both sides are the wrong side of the bed.
But the whispers of your smile
Murmur to my heart a while,
And make the wrong side right for me,
Make the colors bright for me,
Put my dreams in sight for me instead.

Hot and Cold

Don't know what you want.
Yeah, should I stay or should I go,
One day you treat me wrong
And the next you love me so...
I can't tell no more
If I'm high or I'm low.
I still want you so bad,
But you're too hot and too cold.

You say you really want me,
You need me by your side.
But just when we start rollin'
You take me for a ride...
I can't read the signs,
If they're stop or they're go.
I still want you so bad,
But you're too hot and too cold.

Monday you are this.
Tuesday you are that.
By Friday night your lovin's right
But Saturday's all bad...

I can't hear no more,
If it's yes or it's no.
I still want you so bad,
But you're too hot and too cold.

Don't know what you want,
Yeah, should I stay or should I go,
One day you treat me wrong
And the next you love me so...
I can't tell no more
If I'm high or I'm low.

I still want you so bad,
But you're too hot and too cold.
I still need you so bad,
But you're too hot and too cold.
I still got it so bad,
But you're too hot and too cold.

Doin' the Hurly Burly

Oh, it's early, early in the morning,
I shoulda been long in bed.
But I'm still not home,
I'm still out roaming.
Think I'll have a last drink instead.

Oh, the rising sun is shining bright,
Yeah, I shoulda been fast asleep.
But the party was fun
And the night seemed young.
Guess I figured sleeping would keep.

Oh, it's grand to be
So single and so free.
So wake-up-late-and-stay-up-early.
Can't resist when
The fellas/ladies all insist
We go out dancing,
Do the hurly burly.

I don't want to know the consequence,
Don't wanna break my fall.
'Cause tomorrow will stay
One whole day away.
That's when I will wake up,
God, where is my/her make-up?
Guess I'll give the fellas/ladies a call.

The Only Road

I met a girl in high school and thought I fell in love.
Cute and fun and gentle like I'd been dreaming of.
But things all turned out different til I almost lost my mind.
Still it's the only road that I could seem to find.

I dropped out of my college and went into the world.
I planned on doin' this and that and givin' fame a whirl.
But things all turned out different til I almost lost my mind.
Still it's the only road that I could seem to find.

Then she came into my life and then she went away.
My second wife came after her and settled in to stay.
But things all turned out different til I almost lost my mind.
Still it's the only road that I could seem to find.

By now I'm maybe wiser after years in life's hard school.
More of this and less of that have made me less a fool.
But if things still turn out different I'll just have to face the grind.
'Cause it's the only road that I can seem to find.

If Ya Help Someone

If ya help someone, ya know ya help yourself!
If ya help someone, ya know ya help yourself!
If ya share what ya have and ya share who you are,
You'll start to shine like the brightest star.
If ya help someone, ya know ya help yourself!

If ya hurt someone, ya know ya hurt yourself!
If ya hurt someone, ya know ya hurt yourself!
If ya don't really care and ya just wanna fight,
Then ya'll keep feeling wrong and you'll never feel right.
If ya hurt someone, ya know ya hurt yourself!

Giving can make ya feel happy!
Giving can make ya feel glad!
Fighting just makes ya feel angry!
So why make yourself feel angry and mad,
When you can start feeling happy and glad?

If ya help someone, ya know ya help yourself!
If ya help someone, ya know ya help yourself!
If ya share what ya have and ya share who you are,
You'll start to feel … like a movie star!
If ya help someone, ya know ya help yourself!
Yeah, if ya help someone, ya know ya help yourself!!

Little Sister, Pretty Sister

She's a cute little girl,
Small scar on her face.
But there's a much bigger scar
In a much deeper place.

'Cause at school some kids love
To make fun of that scar.
We all know how mean
Some schoolkids just are.

Lots of other ones,
they stand around and they laugh.
While their bullying about
Tears my sister in half.

So this cute little girl,
Small scar on her face,
She comes home to me, crying.
Her only safe place.

Little sister, pretty sister,
You don't need to cry.
'Cause those kids can't hurt you
Right now if they try.

Just know that I love you.
Feel my arms hold you tight.
Little sister, pretty sister,
They're wrong and you're right.

Sometimes I just wonder
What makes some kids mean.
If they really could know you
They'd see what I've seen.

You're a beautiful child
With a beautiful heart.
I won't let a few bullies
Just break you apart.

Little sister, pretty sister,
You don't need to cry.
'Cause those kids can't hurt you
Right now if they try.

Just know that I love you.
Feel my arms hold you tight.
Little sister, pretty sister,
They're wrong and you're right.

Little sister, pretty sister,
They're wrong and you're right.
Little sister, pretty sister,
They're so wrong and you're right

The Ballad of Jack & Sondra

Put on a football suit for our first meeting,
Felt it was her special guy that I was greeting.
The wedding day came and I got to wear a tux,
The days ahead with J&S would surely be deluxe.

Jack and Sondra, Sondra and Jack,
Every time I leave 'em I want to hurry back.
Jack and Sondra, Sondra and Jack,
They're the funnest couple that we'll ever know!

He showed me how to camp and he showed me how to ski,
Then he pulled me off a chairlift to prevent an injury.
We climbed up a mountain and got caught in a cold rain,
But I remember smiling big and feeling no real pain.

Christmas in Vermont, the best there ever were!
All her pies and cookies warmed those freezing temperatures.
And summer family visits and eating too much corn,
When I was at their Essex place I never felt forlorn!

Jack and Sondra, Sondra and Jack,
Every time I leave 'em I want to hurry back.
Jack and Sondra, Sondra and Jack,
They're the funnest couple that we'll ever know!

Kerri, Brad and Erin growing up around this time.
When we lived nearby our dinner visits were sublime.
So when they moved far south I thought they'd maybe
flipped.
But I brought my wives and girlfriends there on many many
trips!

Me-can-no-pay for mansions but we met there anyway.
Lots of laughs in rockers til some gators swam our way.

Still Lake Wheeler's my true favorite 'cause it helps to clear
my head
And I adore it most when I'm in the guest room bed.

Jack and Sondra, Sondra and Jack,
Every time I leave 'em I want to hurry back.
Jack and Sondra, Sondra and Jack,
They're the funnest couple that we'll ever know!
Yes, the funnest couple that we'll ever know!
For sure, the funnest couple that we'll ever know!

Childhood Christmases

When Christmas is here
celebrating each year
sometimes gets in my way.

Decorating the house,
buying gifts for the spouse,
and those credit card bills to pay.

Fighting all the hurried crowds,
relatives who talk too loud,
sizes that are always wrong,
who has time for Christmas songs?

And yet something special remains...

Candles whispering spiced perfume
all around our living room.
Squinting at the Christmas tree made
fairylands of lights to see.

It was magic,
simple magic,
all those childhood Christmases.
They were magic,
simply magic,
all those childhood Christmases

Opening one gift Christmas eve,
the special box I couldn't leave.
Chocolate fudge and Christmas cake
and all those cookies sister baked.

It was magic,
simple magic,
all those childhood Christmases.
They were magic,
simply magic,
all those childhood Christmases.
Remember listening half the night
to make sure Santa got things right?
And wondering how he managed to drop
down your skinny chimney top?

Today it seems so far away
with all those Christmas bills to pay.
But still if I will only pause
I may yet hear old Santa Clause.

It was magic,
simple magic,
all those childhood Christmases.
They were magic,
simply magic,
all those childhood Christmases.
Long ago magical Christmases,
remembering my childhood Christmases.

Sondra's Rap

Yo, some say 60's old,
but they ain't really smart.
By redwood standards you jus'
a young upstart.

And remember sea turtles,
they live 300 years,
so put away all o' them
ol' old-age fears!

And jus' be very glad
ya ain't no Hereford cow,
'cause you'd a been hamburger
for 40 years now.

Yeah, always keep in mind
these words I ain't told ya yet,
(though ya may not recall
what ya ain't s'posed to forget).

Gonna run advice past ya
and I'll run it real slow.
'Cause it's hard to catch some words
when hearin' starts to go.

Some people cough on their coffee,
some people sneeze at a breeze.
And some worry 'bout their heart
and their head and their knees.

Some people sit and watch TV
til their life's watched away,
some people talk about nothin'
til they got nothin' to say.

Some folks is young in years,
yeah, should be young and bold,
and they'd be real young
if they wasn't so old.

People say we only old,
just as old as we feel.
If that cliche means somethin'
don't mean nothin' that's real.
Let's get some water balloons
and play some childish hijinx,
'cause the truth is, Sis,
we only old as we *think*.

So don't worry 'bout them turtles
or the cows or the trees.
Don't worry about that heart
or your head or them knees.

'Sides, ya can't be too old,
nah, turnin' 60 can't be.
'Cause, whoa, 60's only
10 years older than me!

Romance in Fort Lauderdale

I found romance in Fort Lauderdale
Under the swaying palms.
I took a chance that the ocean breeze
would carry my own love songs.

Walking to a golden moon
That rose on the sandy shore,
Kissed by a lovely tune
That promised romance once more.

The sultry sensuous languor
Where summer never ends
Seduces us to fall in love,
Helps broken hearts to mend.
Where endless sea meets endless sky
And sunshine twilights into stars,
Gentle surf caresses gentle shore
And the lovelight's never far.

So I found romance in Fort Lauderdale
As moonglow gave way to sunbright.
I held hands along the soft-sand beach
In this place where love always feels right,
Yes, in this place where love always feels right.

More or Less

(A Simple Verse for Children – and Other People)

Won't make me weak
To help make you strong.
Won't make me short
To help make you long.

Won't make me wrong
To help make you right.
Won't make me loose
To help make you tight.

Won't make me fall
To help make you rise.
Won't make me dumb
To help make you wise.

Won't make me hurt
To help make you heal.
Won't make me fake
To help make you real.

Wish I had known
About this before.
Won't make me less
To help make you more.

Let's Take A Walk

(For George)

I can't be you
I can't free you
You can't be me
But we both can see
We should talk
Maybe take a walk

You've a different face
And you're a different race
From a different place
But still it's the case that
We should talk
Maybe take a walk

Why should we live so lonely
Not even saying hello
When a few words from me to you
Will make us strangers no more?
It's true that I've never met you
And you've never met me
But all the space between us now
Gets small so easily

It just so happens you're here
Happens you're standing so near
I'm not playing some game
Just making sure we're the same
So we should talk
Maybe take a walk
Yes, we should talk
And maybe take a walk
Why don't we talk
As we're taking a walk?

Hear Your Children Call!

(A children's anthem)

We call respect for all, all, all!
We call respect for all, all, all!

Hear your children call, call, call!

We call respect for all, all, all!

POETIC FABLES

The Tale of the Invisible Butterfly

How does it happen that a butterfly becomes invisible?

Invisibility attends beauty more often than you may think, my friend, a cloak that often hides the unique beauties, the profound beauties of this world. True beauty noticed by no one. Yes, it happens around us every day – and not only to butterflies.

So you may find some small interest in this small story of one smallish yellow butterfly who outgrew her yellow smallishness. And as she turned beautiful, uniquely and profoundly beautiful, she instantly became invisible.

You see, when the butterfly first had emerged from the chrysalis her smallish wings appeared ordinary enough. Even to her own new eyes, yes, her new butterfly wings looked a faded yellow that resembled the discolored paper of an old book. (She would learn of this resemblance after flying past humans who were reading discolored old books.)

Faded-paper yellow or not, the butterfly noticed that everyone noticed her. For some reason.

Children would follow the faded butterfly as she butterflew through the garden. Adults would smile as the faded butterfly landed on pentas and passionflowers to sip flower nectar or to lay her eggs. Other faded yellow butterflies danced with her mid-air. Mockingbirds warbled medleys of tunes and squirrels chuckled their approval whenever the smallish faded yellow butterfly appeared.

Oh yes, everyone noticed her then: A yellow butterfly that looked just pretty enough to look the same as all the other yellow butterflies looked in that garden. Like them, she had been predictably, comfortably, unremarkably pleasant to have around. Yes, everyone noticed her then.

But after two weeks of smallish faded yellow-colored life, this particular butterfly began to change. And so did the behavior of everything and everyone around her. For some reason.

Those smallish drab-yellowed wings widened and thickened and soon took on new shades and new hues with each new day that came and went. The butterfly had grown into a cascade of purples and oranges, of blues and greens, at once subtle and vibrant, shimmering as she floated through stands of garden sunlight for everyone to admire.

The butterfly watched herself becoming something nobody could have predicted. Something unique. Something profound.

Something no one could see.

But why? How does it happen that beauty is visible in inverse proportion to its depth and singularity? The deeper and the more unlikely its qualities, the harder to observe.

Ah, that question is one of the curious questions of this life. The obvious beauties are welcomed, the deeper beauties are most often ignored. For some reason.

Or perhaps they are simply unseen. That surely was the case in this case of the invisible butterfly.

Yes, the children who had followed and the adults who had smiled no longer saw the butterfly flying at all. No faded yellow butterflies danced with her mid-air. No mockingbirds warbled, no squirrels chuckled in the garden when she appeared all vibrant and shimmering in the sunlight.

No one noticed any part of her deepening beauty. And the invisible butterfly felt sad from this. She felt very very sad. For what good was an unnoticed butterfly?

During days and long days more, the invisible butterfly nonetheless butterfloated invisibly through the garden. Sipping her nectar and laying her eggs, each day vibrating more colorfully beneath the sunlight. Still unwatched and still unappreciated, of course. And still sad, very very sad because she was so very very beautiful.

It is a sadness that may ring familiar to some who come across this small tale, whether or not they live in a garden.

The invisible butterfly soon felt so sad that she felt as if she never wanted to fly again. No one could see how beautiful she was, no one cared whether she flew through the garden. What did it matter anyway?

Until she remembered something, until she remembered two somethings really.

Yes, the invisible butterfly remembered that she sipped her nectar and remembered also that she laid her eggs. And each day she did this, the garden was becoming a little prettier than the day before. Because she was there.

After all, even an invisible butterfly carries pollen from flower to flower, plant to plant, so that more flowers and plants will grow. And even an invisible butterfly's eggs turn into caterpillars that turn into more butterflies, mostly into butterflies completely and fully visible to everyone.

Maybe it did matter, after all.

Maybe nobody ever would know which butterfly had helped grow the flowers and plants, which butterfly had made so many of those very visible butterflies. But everyone would see the garden as it became a little prettier each new day.

And maybe that's all anything uniquely and profoundly and invisibly beautiful can ever hope to do.

And maybe that's enough.

Moral: Though no one may understand us as we truly are, our efforts to help others make a difference.

The Tale of the Yellowbright Flower

Flowers feel feelings. Strong emotions vibrating out through their stamens and pistils. It's a secret well known by flower lovers who coax blooms open with whispered encouragements. So it should be no surprise that the Yellowbright Flower growing in a large red field trembled with feelings now. Yes, he trembled each day from the strong feelings he felt. He felt different, after all, which is always a strong and unsettling thing to feel. He was the only Yellowbright Flower flowering in a field of red something-or-other plants. Whatever they were. He knew walkers walking by stopped walking and wondered at the sight of the Yellowbright Flower, stopped and stared before walking on. He knew he was some special thing, the only thing of his kind. But so what? Because the only thing of anything is always a very lonely thing to be, no matter what thing it is.

Until one midnight moonful lightbright night, as the Yellowbright Flower bobbed on a summer wind, the field spoke to him. Yes, a voice came from the field itself, from one red something-or-other plant itself in the field itself. This plant, whatever it was, now spoke to the Yellowbright Flower by saying this: "You're not really alone, you know." No one and nothing had ever spoken to the Yellowbright Flower before. To say the Yellowbright Flower was startled would be an understatement. Remember, flowers feel strong feelings.

"You've missed it all along," the red plant went on to the Yellowbright Flower. "You're a rose. So am I. So are we all, all of us in this big field. If you're yellow, with a different bloom, your color only adds to the beauty of this field. But it's all of us, together, that the walkers stop walking to see. Not just you. Together, we're a garden. Alone, you're only one pretty but very small blossom." Funny how this changed things for the Yellowbright Flower, who now recognized he was really a

Yellowbright Rose. Funny how those few words changed everything. Because no thing is really the only thing of anything, no matter how special that one thing is. Somehow it helps to feel this when you're a flower feeling strong feelings. Yes, somehow a flower garden just feels like a much less lonely place to flower, don't you think?

MORAL: We stop feeling isolated when we understand we're part of something larger than ourselves.

The Tale of Generous Jen

Upon some time lived Jennifer once. Writing a children's book, she was, all in lovely scented verse. Writing only once, perhaps twice, a month. Perhaps. When she could find some time.

This was how Jennifer's scented children's book began:

"Music comes alive at night, you know.

Every note has ears to hear.

It listens for the first sound of your snore.

And waits for your dreams to come near."

Enchanted imagination was Jennifer's great gift, telling us of things no one else could think to tell. Much more than these few lovely words, oh yes, Jennifer had almost written. But all the rest was still locked inside her head, just dancing and humming to get out for some young someone-else to read.

Just when Jennifer's words would be unlocked free, oh my – this was anyone's guess. If those words would ever be unlocked at all. Because Jennifer was so generous, you see. "Generous Jen," her family all called her. Jen's fingertips were usually far too busy helping someone else with something else for those fingertips to unlock her enchanted imagination. Whether that help for someone else was needed much or not.

No matter how many other fingertips were busy baking cookies for the church bake sale, Generous Jen always volunteered her fingertips too. No matter that her mother rarely wore some pair of worn pants – Generous Jen hemmed them up some half-inch higher with her busy fingertips. Just in case her mother changed her mind. Every friend who didn't really need help packing up to move got Jennifer's generous help anyway.

Every friend of a friend who didn't really need a ride to the airport got their ride anyway from Generous Jen.

There was not a "no" bone in her body any time anyone hinted they might prefer a "yes" from Jennifer. Always giving, giving, giving something or other to someone who didn't really need her smallish gifts. That was Generous Jennifer.

If that's what real giving really means, of course.

Because some gifts are gifts much easier to give than others, perhaps. Perhaps.

Much easier to give, at least, than writing scented verses.

MORAL: Society benefits most when each individual shares their greatest gifts.

The Tale of the Green Grass

It was a green lawn, a very green lawn, a green green lawn. And big. Yes, it was the first green lawn to grow green on the very first day of spring. A broad expanse of grass that covered a broad expanse of rich topsoil in an awakening springtime world.

Very big. Very green.

On this very first day of spring, every blade of grass in this green lawn felt a justifiable sense of pride. Each blade knew it was one part of something very big and very green. Each blade looked around just to admire the sight of it all. And each blade would have smiled at that sight if blades of grass had lips. Because a very green lawn on the very first day of spring is a sight worth seeing, as everyone who has seen such a sight surely agrees.

Yes, every single blade of green grass was smiling somewhere within. Because every single blade of green grass could feel itself standing up tall and high and proud on this day, each blade equally important, each blade contributing its own special green something to the whole vast greenness of the big green lawn.

This special green pride continued for a whole day, almost.

Right up until one green blade of grass decided it was taller than the others. The tall blade could see the tops of those other puny green blades far below, perhaps a full inch lower to the ground. Right away, the tall blade understood exactly what this meant: One blade of grass was more special than the others. Oh yes, the tall blade knew that it was the most special single blade of grass on that vast big whole green lawn.

The tall blade of grass began to feel entitled. Entitled to more minerals from the topsoil around it, entitled to more rain from the sky when the rain began to fall later during that very first lovely spring day. It was obvious, very obvious, that the tall blade was entitled.

Obvious to all, perhaps, but the other blades of grass growing all around the tall blade.

Now, one by one, each blade began to feel entitled too. Entitled to more than the other blades growing all around it. Entitled to more of the minerals in the rich topsoil. Entitled to more of the rain that fell from the sky.

Sure, because this blade decided it was a prettier green than any of the others. And that blade decided it was broader and stronger than the other blades of grass. And then still another grassy blade decided its roots were growing deepest into the topsoil. And on it went, oh sure, on and on and on it all went. One blade of green grass after another blade after still another blade, each one deciding it had some special quality more special than any of the others.

This deciding spread throughout the big green lawn during the very first day of spring and the second and third and fourth days of spring that followed. Yes, oh sure, this kind of deciding often spreads very fast.

Each blade wondered over and over to itself, "Why can't the others see how special I am?"

Right up until the tall blade of grass stopped deciding and wondering such things for a moment. And took another good look around.

The entire lawn was brown now. Light brown expanses that looked like straw mixed among dirty dark brown blotches, all dry despite all the springtime rain. Oh sure, yes, that vast big whole lawn somehow had nearly dried itself dead. Somehow.

The tall blade of grass stopped feeling any sense of pride. So did the pretty green blade and the strong, broad blade and the deep-rooted blade. (Though, in truth, those blades no longer were so tall or pretty or broad or deep-rooted anymore.) Every blade of grass on that big big brown brown lawn soon felt very different than before.

And each blade began to wonder to itself, "What is wrong?"

This was just before the tall blade of grass dipped his tall blade to offer the pretty green blade below a big sip of rain water, yes, rain water that had collected on the tall blade. And this inspired the pretty green blade to tilt just enough to share that water with the strong, broad blade. Which, in turn, shared that water with the deep-rooted blade.

Now many of the other blades of grass, sure, lots of other blades began to share their rain water with one another too. Seeing this, still other blades of grass on the big lawn pulled in their roots just enough – enough, that is, to allow the blades nearby to draw more of the minerals from the rich black topsoil.

And on it went, oh sure, on and on and on it all went. One blade of grass after another blade after still another blade, each one deciding it would share something with the other blades of grass nearby.

This deciding spread from one blade to another to another and on and on to still others, yes, spreading throughout the big lawn during the fifth and sixth and seventh days of spring that followed. Funny but, yes, this kind of deciding sometimes can spread even faster than the other kinds.

And on the seventh day, the tall blade of grass took another good look around again. Looking all around at the vast lawn that spread all all around everywhere, the tall blade felt a greater sense of pride than ever before in its tall grassy life.

The entire lawn was green again. Full and thick, very big and very green.

Oh yes, the tall blade understood now that each blade on that big vast green lawn was one part of something very big and something very green. Each blade somehow different in some way or some other way. But each blade in some way contributing its own important green something.

The tall blade would have smiled at that thought if blades of grass had lips.

MORAL: We each grow best when we recognize that we're part of something larger than ourselves.

The Tale of Almost Alvin

Alvin held high high expectations. Expectations for every he or she that he knew, including the he that was he, Alvin.

High expectations were not an easy thing to hold, not a joyful thing to hold. No. Because it was sad yet truthful to say that not one single he or she ever quite lived up to Alvin's high expectations, including the he that was he, Alvin. Especially that he, yes that he most of all.

Sad, sad.

Each day Alvin tried it all all over again. Oh sure, he went out into the world of shes and hes all over again with hopes held high high, expecting to find the perfect someone else to like, somewhere-somehow. Surely there was one she somewhere who happily would listen and listen whenever he spoke every anything at all, a she who would converse only in smart (and brief) remarks, a she who would prove most charmful and most loveful and who craved to cook for Alvin, yes, to cook very very well.

And surely there was a he somehow who would just want to pal around, yes, around whenever and wherever Alvin wanted a pal, a he who would prove a loyal buddy and a best most generous friend.

But no and no. No such she or he ever quite turned up as the days and years shimmered past Alvin.

Almost, yes, almost sometimes – every now and then. Until the new disappointment set in and another almost friend was lost.

There was the she who worked in the same office building as Alvin, smart and pretty and fun, a she who even craved to cook for Alvin and cooked very very well. They had smart and pretty fun together for some weeks until Alvin suddenly saw some something in she that he had not quite seen until that moment. No, no, this was a she who just talked way too much.

And there was the he who lived in the same condo building as Alvin, a he who wanted a pal and loyal buddy as much as Alvin did. He was a he who always paid more than his share and who always was ready to pal and buddy around at the drop of an instant. They spent many an evening as pals and buddies around and around for some months. Until Alvin suddenly realized something in he that Alvin had not quite realized until that particular instant. No, no, this was a he who was not very smart.

Almost, yes, so close each time. But each time, just in time, Alvin was smart enough to figure these people out before it was too late.

And so, after each almost-time, Alvin had time enough at home alone to further explore his own set of shortcomings, his inadequacies and inconsistencies, his traits that were too much and his abilities that were too little. Oh, yes, Alvin was no less relentless in finding his own lag and lack, the lackluster among a stream of his seeming strengths. No, no, Alvin did not fool Alvin one bit.

For whenever he looked, really looked, for his own failings among those high high expectations, he always found more than one something to see. There was his receding hairline, for one something, and his pudge of belly fat. There was that nasal voice and that annoying girlish gesture with his right hand.

Alvin also saw that Alvin talked way way too much. And Alvin realized that deep down Alvin wasn't really very smart at all. There just wasn't much about Alvin that Alvin much liked.

Sad, sad. Sad.

Yet each day Alvin tried it all all over again. Oh sure, he went out into the world of shes and hes all over again with hopes held high high, expecting to find the perfect someone else to like at last, somewhere and somehow.

And why not? Because a perfect someone else who liked Alvin in return, perhaps, might help Alvin to like Alvin a little bit too.

Moral: If we want to like ourselves, we must appreciate others despite their imperfections.

The Tale of the Sea Wave

The sea wave knew what happened to sea waves in the end.

They disappeared.

This was the fate of all waves that ever tumbled across the ocean's vast, grand surface. Including him.

When he had been just a little wavelet far out at sea, he had heard the stories, the rumors, the old wave's tales. There was something called the shore. Or so everyone said. The shore was the destroyer of waves, of large waves and small, of frothy waves and gentle waves alike. No wave survived an encounter with this thing called the shore.

Ever.

One fact was certain. Once any wave rolled off past the horizon, it was never seen again. Yes, waves disappeared all right.

The sea wave also recognized, of course, that he was a wave of no special significance. Or so everyone said. No one and nothing was likely to much care when he washed up against some face of rock or shallow of sand ashore – simply one of many, one of uncounted millions to appear on the broad ocean for a moment before vanishing forever.

But he cared, yes, the insignificant sea wave cared. How was it possible any wave simply could cease to exist? What would the end be like? How long would it take? Was it going to hurt? Most of all, what would become of him … you know, afterwards.

These were big questions to ponder, especially for a wave so insignificant as him.

For the first time in his undulating and unimportant life, the sea wave wanted something more. Wanted to understand why he had come and where he would go.

The sea wave's troubled pondering rolled onward with him hour upon hour as he rolled and rolled onward far past the sea's horizon. Until his pondering rolled him to a thought he had never pondered before: The sea wave realized there was something all around him and all under him and all within him too. It was everywhere.

It was water.

And so was he.

He was not just a single small wave undulating upon the surface of the sea. He was the sea and the sea was the water and the water was always.

And so was he.

Waves had come and had gone. He had come and would go. Other waves large and small, frothy and gentle alike would do the same, each swirling into watery existence from the vast, grand surface of the ocean. Each a singular wave yet each wave one part of the vast and the grand that was everywhere, everywhere.

And as he pondered all of this, the small sea wave rolled on now, rolled on joyfully somehow across the vast, grand surface of the ocean. The sea wave simply rolled on.

Moral: When we recognize ourselves as one part of a larger whole, our existence gains significance.

With appreciation to Thich Nhat Hanh: "Enlightenment, for a wave in the ocean, is the moment the wave realizes it is water."

The Tale of the Teller Twins

Everyone in town called them "the twins." Tripp and Terry Teller, identical in all ways – except one. As you will see. The Teller twins were tree trimmers and had a nice little business going too. Chopping at trunks, grinding down roots, thinning out limbs. The twins had grown up around this town and this town had grown up around the twins. Yes, this town was no small place anymore and the Teller boys had no small business either.

Tripp Teller seemed the driving force. It was Tripp with the charm smile and it was Tripp with the glad pat on the shoulder for everyone. Everyone, at least, who might need their trees trimmed. To Tripp Teller, tree trimming served one purpose only: to give him "the good stuff," as he always called it. The good stuff meant the good car and the good house of course. Of course. But most of all the good stuff meant feeling like someone important around town, owner of a good business that was pulling in good money. Of course. Sometimes Tripp almost forgot that his twin brother really was his twin brother – almost forgot that Terry really was his brother at all. The tree trimming business to Tripp was all about "me." Nothing else. Though he had to admit that Terry did help get all those trees trimmed much faster. Which of course allowed Tripp to have more of the good stuff sooner. Of course.

As for Terry, yes, he looked just like Tripp and talked just like Tripp and usually even walked just like Tripp. No one could tell them apart when the twins ambled down Maple Street. But Terry knew the difference between them even if nobody else knew the difference, even if his own brother didn't know the difference either. To Terry Teller, the tree trimming business really wasn't all about "me." Trimming trees somehow was about "us." Yes, trimming trees to Terry was about doing something to help people in that not-small hometown of theirs.

And trimming trees especially was about working side by side with his twin brother Tripp, sharing each day with the person he loved most of all in all their town and in all their world.

This was the one big difference between Terry Teller and his twin brother Tripp Teller. But no one in all their town, or in all their world either, knew about this difference of course. No one except for Terry Teller. To everyone else, the twins were identical in all ways.

Then something happened. There was one big tree in one big wind one night. And the big wind pushed the big tree on to another big tree, which was pushed on to another big tree, and that tree in turn was pushed on another and on and on it all went, trees tumbling like dominos, falling trunk after trunk after trunk after trunk with a crash. A very big crash.

The problem was that all these tree trunks crashed mainly on one house. Yes, all these trees had grown up mainly around one house and now somehow they all had crashed down mainly on that one house too. The trees had crashed down on the house of Tripp Teller.

As luck or unluck would have it, both Tripp and Terry Teller were sitting inside Tripp's home at the time of this crash. They were in the basement going over work schedules for the next day's tree trimming. But now the Teller twins were trapped.

Trunk after trunk after trunk lay on top of the shattered house, which had collapsed on top of the basement.

To top off these problems, the twins had no water or food in the basement. They had no cellphone in their pockets either. And no one could hear them yell for help – Tripp's good house was far too far away from every other house in town, sitting on top of a good tall hill. And all their tree trimming tools were locked inside their tree trimming shop several miles from the home of

Tripp Teller.

Tripp and Terry had very little at hand to help them. Except for their four hands, of course, and a small knife and a single dull axe tucked in one basement corner. Nothing else.

The first thought that flitted through Tripp Teller's head after the big crash was about "me." Of course. As in, "I'm glad I'm not dead! How am I going to get me out of here?" The first thought that lingered in Terry Teller's head after the big crash was about "us." As in, "I'm so thankful we're not dead! We've got to find some way to get us both out of here!"

But getting out was easier said than done, as they say.

The tree trimming twins hatched a plan of escape, with Terry using the knife to carve deep notches in the fallen tree trunks that had trapped them below the ground and Tripp using the axe to chop at the notched tree trunks. With each carve of the small knife, Terry thought to himself, "We're going to get us both outta here!" With each chop of the dull axe, Tripp thought to himself, "I'm getting me outta here!"

They carved and chopped for many hours but eventually night spilled into the next day and that next day soon spilled into another night and on and on it all went. Until a terribly tired Tripp at last thought to himself, "No more. I don't care anymore if I get out of here! I give up!"

But you'll remember that there was one big difference between Terry Teller and his twin brother Tripp Teller. As Tripp Teller soon discovered at last.

Terry Teller was tired too, of course, just as tired as Tripp. Or maybe more, maybe. But the thought now foremost in Terry's mind was this: "Tripp needs to rest a while but I'm ok. I still can keep working. I'm going to find some way to chop on this tree trunk hard enough to get us both out of here!"

When Terry swung the axe again, he felt an odd feeling. He felt as if the chopping suddenly had become easier somehow. He wasn't sure why. Terry felt as if he felt now for sure that he could chop through that tree trunk. Somehow. It almost felt to Terry as if his hands and arms really didn't feel so tired anymore. Maybe almost as if his hands and arms didn't feel tired at all somehow, maybe.

But how could that be?

Terry Teller didn't stop to wonder. As Tripp drifted asleep, Terry continued chopping with that dull axe, chipping away bit by bit by bit through the thick tree trunk. He may as well have been trying to dig through a concrete wall with a small spoon. But Terry kept chopping and chipping at that trunk until even a dull axe proved strong enough at last – strong enough, at least, when it was swung by two untired hands and arms.

And if such strange strength seems to you like something that happens only in fables, think again. Look again. It is all around you every day, somewhere in your town sometimes. Maybe it is inside you too, sometimes, when you're not looking. Whatever. But it happens. It does happen. Really. Just ask Terry Teller.

So, yes, Terry at last chopped through one thick tree trunk with that dull axe, then used that broken trunk as a lever to shift aside another tree trunk, then awakened his brother so they could squeeze through the narrow opening together to safety. The twins were free. Hungry, thirsty, tired and shaken but free again.

And when Tripp Teller, still dazed, stood in the free air outside to look at his shattered home and then over at his smiling twin brother, he could only think to ask a simple question: "How did you do that, Terry? How could you do that alone?"

And when Terry Teller looked over at his brother at that moment, he could only think of one simple answer: "I didn't do it alone, Tripp. I couldn't have done it alone, you're right. We did it, brother – together."

MORAL: One man working only for himself struggles alone. But one man working for himself and others discovers the strength of many.

The Tale of No-Time Nora

No, no, no, no! No was No-Time Nora's favorite word. Often she would say, while hurrying past him or her in some frantic flurry, "No! Sorry! No time!" No time for coffee with a colleague. Sorry! No time for sewing with her sister. Sorry! No time for a film with a friend. Sorry! No, nor time to stop and listen, nor time to stop and chat. Nora was far too busy for frivolous stuff, for time-wasting things like that.

"Sorry, sorry, sorry! Gotta go feed the dog! And then the cat," she would blurt into her cellphone while darting door to door, car to apartment, in very few seconds. Usually just 26 seconds flat. Though with her arms loaded with grocery bags, Nora would sometimes wave one spare finger, very quickly, toward her neighbors Paula, Spencer and Nat.

No-Time Nora had showers to scour, you see. Washing to wash, dusting to dust. Endless errands, a list of things-to-do that filled up her day. Important stuff, time-taking chores like that. And when they were done, just before bed, there was always the company of her dog. And her cat.

There was no time at all for doing with others. There just were not two seconds in her day to give two seconds to anyone at all. She never could squeeze in one instant for friendly frolics or friendships, she never could eek out one moment for moments of family fun. Though sometimes Nora paused long enough to admire her checklists showing all the chores she just got done.

Of course, none of Nora's "no's" was entirely necessary. Her shower was completely mildew-free. Even her dog was scrubbed down and her cat was washed clean. As were Nora's doors and windows and every one of her window screens.

But at least her busywork life kept her so, so, so busy. So busy she had almost no time to notice how busy she was being unhappy. No-Time Nora just numbly buzzed with a busy loneliness throughout each busywork day. With no one and nothing in her busy life but one fat dog. And one very fat cat. And one sparkling shower – oh yes, and also one totally spotless white bathmat.

Until one day, Nat helped Nora with an armload of groceries, smiled and said to her, "Nora, my neighbor, some of us plan to help out another neighbor who needs some real help this weekend, just down the street. I know you're always rushing off to do chores in a frantic flurry. But why not help us help our neighbor for just two hours – or just one hour's helping if you really have to hurry?"

She could at last meet all the nice neighbors in their nice neighborhood, Nat told Nora. Giving two of her busy hours to someone else might make her smile more than she seemed to smile now. She could set aside for a while, Nat suggested, all the endless chores of her frantic, flurried life. Nora might even talk a bit with Spencer and Paula – who, Nat explained, were his son and his wife.

Nora pondered Nat's invitation for just a moment. For two seconds Nora gave his suggestion a first and second thought. Maybe she really needed to meet some people. Maybe doing something for somebody else would do her some good. Maybe a nice smile with some nice neighbors would make a nice change. And with Paula and Spencer, she might even have some pleasant words to exchange.

But you know, of course, how No-Time Nora answered Nat. "No" was the first of the few short words in her no-time reply. "No time for helping neighbors, but thanks, Nat – goodbye!"

Sometime later, after Nat was gone, Nora told herself she really would like to help her needy neighbor. Why, of course she would! Because she was a giving person after all. If, if, if only there were more hours in her busy, busy day. But on the big neighbor-helping weekend, of course, she really had to scrub down the dog and clean up the cat. "And then there's that dirty shower to scour," Nora reminded herself, "and I really, really must wash that filthy white bathmat!"

Time for sharing herself with others was time that No-Time Nora always seemed to lack. Besides, when she had tried sharing herself with others, in the long ago past, others sometimes didn't share themselves back. Life was so, so much simpler with just her one sparkling shower and her one fat dog – and her one very fat cat.

MORAL: Sharing ourselves with others is essential to a full, meaningful life.

The Tale of the Two Windows

Look!

Two windows.

In different rooms.

Both above the playground.

With children outdoors, many laughters.

Together they joyful play.

Or maybe not.

Most curious …

Look!

Oh yes, yes, oh yes yes yes yes yes. This was a scene most indeed curious to see, this was yes indeed.

Waldo had seen this curiosity indeed now for some many months or more. And each time Waldo saw, oh yes, the curiosity caught his breath up in some snort of surprisement yet again.

Two windows. Different rooms, yes, same scene below.

Or maybe not.

Hmmmmm …

You see, Waldo's curious seeings started something like this, yes, just exactly like this those seeings began. Because Waldo woke up on one extrashiny morning as the sun in narrow lightslivers slipped between his slatted blinds, all the new day's brightlight filtering inside among the slats to poke Waldo awake warmly on both his sleeping eyelids.

Despite this distinctly sunwarmed wakening, Waldo soon felt distinctly unsunny.

Scowling and scratching the scruffy mornstubble of his beard, he pulled a thin white cord to raise the slatted blinds of the bedroom window. Peering squinteyed through the sunwarmth, Waldo peeked down at a playground mostly unsunny to see, oh yes a playscene below quite plainly playless.

Oh no, oh yes yes indeed.

The unplaying children smiled little, smiled hardly at all. Quite listless, quite playless, five boys tossed a ball. Four girls just ran round in a small silly ring. Three kids more found some sour song to sing. Two teachers, it seemed, were both bored to tears. And one lost lonely child sat huddled by fears.

Shaking his scowl and scraping his scratch, Waldo unwelcomed the long day ahead – yes the endless workingday at a workingplace not much unlike that playground below him. All the playless hours to come in his unfun office cubicle, with Waldo himself all fullup with feelings quite listless and bored quite to tears. Unwelcome thoughts indeed as Waldo walked a few short steps down the short narrow hallway toward his short kitchen for coffee. Espresso, short.

And then, well, it happened.

Yes, this was when Waldo curiously peeked curiously through the round window in the square kitchen wall. Peeked down at that same playground he'd peeked only one short moment ago, peeked first now then peered next until both his scowl and his scratch had nearly fallen off his face.

He saw five beaming boys, so strong, playing catch. Four girls raced round in a short footrace match. Three choirkids practiced some sweet ancient song. Two teachers both cried from laughing too long. And that boy? He hunched over a big frog that he'd found, a frog hopping happily through that sunwarmed playground.

Hmmmmm …

Two windows. Different rooms, no yes, same scene below.

Or maybe not.

Same ball yes, same running path yes. Same kids, same teachers too. All, all, all, all just exactly the same through this window, then through that.

But then, no, of course the same not at all.

First unhappy below, then happy.

First joyless children, then joyful.

How could just the same all suddenly seem just so different?

Yes, even his hearings had so changed from one window to the next with one same sound sounding so sourly through this, so sweetly through that. Yes, just the same child soundings separated only by short seconds and short footsteps of floor.

Waldo sat down with his coffee, most indeed curiously confused. And he thought back on what had come to him through the two windows.

Unhappy, then happy. Joyless, then joyful.

How curious yes, Waldo wondered during some coffeesipping and then some soapshowering as he prepared for work. All all so curious, yes, it seemed all so curious indeed as Waldo somehow found himself with no scowl at all now, no scratch at all either. And then undreading the long day ahead, he soon hustled off to his workingplace through the sunwarmth outside.

And so things went on for some many months or more. First seeing this, then seeing that outside his two windows. Hearing sourly hearings here, followed by sweetly hearings there. Not always only playground children either, but windowseeings and windowhearings of rainstorms and roadtraffic, of songbirds and spanielwalkers.

Each time both scenes outside the two windows just exactly the same.

But each time each scene outside the two windows just exactly as different as each time before.

Here unhappy, there happy.

Here joyless.

There joyful.

Day after day after day, his apartment's two windows revealed two worlds to Waldo. Day after day after day, Waldo never could decide which of these two worlds was true, which world real.

Was it all a place of sadness down below him, grim and grimacing, everyone scowling and scratching to endure the endless unplayful hours? Or was it a place of energies and enthusiasms, with songsweet laughter bubbling effervescent through roadtraffic and rainstorms, all playful to cheer the songbirds and spanielwalkers alike?

Once himself outdoors down below the two windows, Waldo could never decide which was what. Day after day after day Waldo walked down the walk beside the roadtraffic, through the rainstorms, passing beneath the songbirds and passing past the spanielwalkers with Waldo himself all fullup of feelings indeed most curious. And mostly quite confused. Even his cubicled workingplace seemed different now somehow – but why, and how?

The which and the what, the why and the how of it all seemed ever as muddled as ever before.

And then, well, it happened.

Because one day after one day and another day, Waldo found one most curious wondering among the many wonders that wound through Waldo's own head. Yes, one day Waldo himself snorted in surprisement over this most curious wonder: "Maybe both the unhappy and the happy, yes, maybe both were both always there. On the playground, in the rainstorms and the roadtraffic and all the rest. Joyless and joyful both always both just as real! Hmmmm … I wonder why I never noticed before?"

The why and the how and the which and the what of it all, Waldo never could quite explain. But instantly he just knew it was all so. And Waldo would never let himself unknow what the two windows had taught him for some many months or more.

Yes, Waldo always had found just what he wanted to find below a windowpane. No, it was no difference below now making those two windowscenes unsame. He could find the world scowling, much like Waldo's own scowls. Uncuriously all playless with soursongs sounding like howls. Or he could find the world playful with sweetsongs of joys. Curiously no scowlseeings to see with no hearings of noise.

Playless and sour.

Or playful and sweet.

Waldo decided this hour by hour when up looking out windows or down walking the street.

He could hear it all just as noise or could hear it just as all song – and not one of his hearings really was wrong. Just the same with his seeings, both unhappy and happy were real there outside. But which seeings he saw there he'd somehow decide.

A snort of surprisement seems a wise way to react when two different windows show two quite different facts.

Yes, all joyful the play there! Or no, maybe not.

People can only discover outside them, yes, the things inside them they've already got.

Moral: The world always has both good and bad but we decide which one most influences our life.

The Tale of Me-First Mary

Mary was an odd name for this particular Mary. For this particular Mary often pursed her unmerry lips in disgust at some other someone. Someone, anyone who got in her way during any particular day. Mary was as unmerry as any someone could be.

Knowing that she lived in a me-first world, Mary often used her lips to speak aloud the two words always mostly on her mind. "Me." And "my." (Sometimes Mary often spoke the words "I" and "mine" too.) These were the syllables that tumbled off her tongue from each day's first sunflicker to every night's final moongleam.

Driving to work, she fumed that an accident ahead on the highway put "me" behind schedule. Vacationing in the mountains, she snorted that her boyfriend's sprained ankle ruined "my" holiday. Watching television, she sniffed that terrible news about terrible floods somewhere interrupted "my" favorite program. The drivers in the accident and the boyfriend in the mountains and the people living near terrible floods were not tickled by these events either, of course, though this thought never meandered completely into Mary's mind.

Mary wasn't mean, mind you. No, Mary didn't want to hurt anyone, of course, of course not. No, Mary had just learned, oh yes, Mary had learned the big lesson very very well: If you're helping someone else, you're not helping yourself. It was a hard but simple truth, as every someone understood in this me-first world.

The trouble with being just one me in a me-first world is all those other me-firsters living in your world, of course. Yes, all those other me-first people just keep getting in your way. Which was why Mary so often pursed her unmerry lips in disgust at some other someone. Which was why Mary was as unmerry as any someone could be.

And so it went for Me-First Mary, day after day after day becoming less merry by the moment. Until one day Mary had to wonder, just for one moment beneath her pursed unmerry lips: "Maybe me-first isn't the best way to be in this world. Maybe, maybe helping only yourself isn't really helping yourself at all." This is what Mary wondered one day.

Was it possible that doing something helpful for some other someone really might help Mary too somehow? Was it possible Mary might feel a little merrier if she thought a little less about herself alone? Was it really possible that any of this was really possible in this me-first world?

Mary pursed her lips again, tighter than usual.

"No, that's really not possible," Mary said tartly to herself aloud. "My life's hard enough just worrying about 'me' all the time! 'Me,' 'me,' 'me' every minute and I still can't get what I want. Imagine how bad my life would be if I started worrying about any of 'them' too!"

MORAL: Living for ourselves alone is self-defeating

The Tale of the Small Hole

Life is tough if you're nothing but a small hole. For big holes, sure, things aren't quite so bad, sure, sure. At least bigger is better, as everyone knows. But for each small hole poked into the fabric of this world somewhere, there is almost nothing to do but to live in hollow boredom.

The worst of it was this, though: The Small Hole wasn't even sure, totally sure, he was even a hole even. He was round. Sort of. He was empty inside. Kind of. But he sat among rows of black lines on a field of white. His best guess was that he came into being as a tiny hole in a sheet of paper. But he wasn't sure, not totally sure, not sure at all.

The Small Hole had lived all his small vacant life with this terrible uncertainty. Big holes at least had some purpose anyway. They could let big things pass through them anyway, like a tunnel that is a pass-through for cars anyway. At least it was something to do with your day. Even some small holes could be useful sometimes, it seemed, as when a finger scratches an itchy leg through the pocket hole of old jeans. Even small holes had a purpose even, sometimes. Not a grand purpose, mind you. But amid the nothingness of small hole life, even small purposes were welcome.

So sat the Small Hole, day after day. Round and empty, sort of, kind of. Unable even to think of himself as a big nothing even, because he was only a small nothing after all. The Small Hole had no purpose and nothing to give at all.

Or so it seemed.

Until the day he overheard one voice uttering some very interesting words. (Yes, holes can understand whatever people say. Most recognize several languages as well as signing for the deaf.) The Small Hole heard one man's voice talking, followed by very beautiful sounds. The same voice again, then more sounds of a beauty the Small Hole had never heard before. And then once more, the same man's voice again, once more yes the same man's voice, but now very loud, very bellowy now. This is when the man's words got very interesting, if also very loud.

"You're late!" the man's voice bellowed. "You have the most important moment in this whole work – and you're late! Play on the downbeat, as it is written!"

The Small Hole understood the words, of course, but he could not make sense of their true meaning. What was the bellowing man talking about? Soon enough, the Small Hole would learn.

Because now the voice of the bellowing man continued: "I can't believe my ears! One note to play and you get it wrong! That cymbal crash is the climax of this great symphony by this great composer and you cannot be late! On the downbeat, Mr. Nada! It's right here on your page! Let me show you! Let me mark your score so you can't miss it again!"

What was the bellowing man saying? The Small Hole glanced quickly around now, excited. Because something was happening now. Yes, now the bellowing man was standing near him, drawing a circle in pencil now. A circle around … him! Around the Small Hole! The bellowing man was drawing a circle around the Small Hole, which of course meant the bellowing man had been talking about the Small Hole!

And now the Small Hole suddenly understood something he never had understood before. Something that made everything make sense at last. Because the Small Hole was not a hole at all after all, after all. He was a musical note. Sitting in the middle of a sheet of lined music paper, all alone. All alone – because he was so important.

"The most important moment in this whole work," the bellowing man, who really was the orchestra conductor, had called the Small Hole. "The climax of this great symphony by this great composer," the bellowing orchestra conductor man had added. Then the bellowing conductor had drawn that circle in pencil around him, around the Small Hole.

Yes, the Small Hole understood now for sure, for sure. He wasn't a Small Hole. He was a Big Note. He was the Big Note that made the cymbals of the orchestra crash loudly together at just the right time at just the right place in the music for everyone in the audience to enjoy. For sure, the most important musical note in this great symphony by this great composer!

And the Big Note understood one thing more, for sure. He understood that this is how it goes sometimes, for sure, for sure. Because sometimes we are sitting just a little too close to the page to see everything, that's all. Sometimes it all looks just too big all around us to recognize our real place among it all, that's all.

Sometimes we have a more important purpose, much more important, than we think. Yes, this is what the Big Note understood at last. Except sometimes we just need someone to draw a circle around us, in pencil, to show us what we were missing all along.

MORAL: Each of us has an important purpose once we recognize it for ourselves.

The Tale of Techie Tom

Thomas was a technical type. Totally. His colleagues in IT called him TT. To them, he was "Techie Tom." But he felt sure all the Ts in his nickname were merely a teasing for him, initials given not with affection but with disdain. His colleagues didn't really like him, TT would think each day. No one wanted him around. Except for his whiz-bang wizardry on the Internet, he was a man of little interest and lesser use to anybody. Or so TT thought.

Eating lunch this day, alone as usual and thinking typically techie things, TT picked up a magazine. One article instantly caught his attention. "The Humanity Project helps people live more happily through learning to give to others," the story read. TT scratched his earlobe and other parts. A bit of smelly tuna was stuck to his lip when he lowered the magazine and said out loud, to himself only, "What does that mean anyway? That's stupid! What do I have to give anyone?"

But TT kept turning the magazine pages. Because the magazine article next said, "The Humanity Project teaches us to focus our actions and thoughts on giving all we can to others each day, without expecting reward or fearing rejection. This 'giving life' connects our daily individual efforts to something larger than any one person: humanity. And that can help bring us each greater meaning and happiness." Now TT was terribly troubled. In an untypically testy display of emotion, he tossed the magazine to the table and stalked angrily from the lunchroom. "'A giving life!'" he tsked and snorted over and over, walking back to his safe, separate cubicle.

On the way, TT passed two techie colleagues talking about music or something. He never listened to anyone's untechie chatter and heard not two words. So he did not overhear one colleague telling the other that they'd never find a drummer for their weekend jazz trio. Of course, TT had played the drums all through high school. Still had a drum set hidden in his closet. "'A giving life!'" TT snorted again as he walked past.

TT still tsked and snuffled as he passed Theresa's cubicle, who looked up from her techie tinkering long enough to sigh to herself, "TT's such a cute guy! Too bad he doesn't like anyone around here." Then she watched him stalk past her and she got a funny, sad, if-only look in her two eyes. Down the techie hall, TT closed his ears again and hurried by someone who was touring techie cubicles collecting donations for some good cause or other that didn't concern him anyway. Back within his safe, separate cubicle space now, TT did not phone his mother who was ill or his older sister who missed his voice or his younger brother who had always admired him. And TT, who loved and understood baseball, did not make plans to coach a Little League team that season or support the local major leaguers by attending even one game. After all, TT had a TV. And after work, TT did not take his seriously major techie talents down the street to the struggling school with all the broken computer terminals. The list of did-nots is too long to list here, in toto. Instead, TT fired up a microwave pizza, alone at home as usual, and turned on the ballgame. "'A giving life!'" TT tsked one last time, to himself. "I've got nothing at all to give. And even if I did, who would want it anyway?"

MORAL: Each individual has something important to share with others.

About the Author

Robert Spencer Knotts is the author of 26 previous published books, most of these for young readers and written under the name Bob Knotts or a pseudonym. He also has written five plays, numerous poems, fables, blogs, lyrics and other literary works. In addition, Knotts is a lifelong musician who has composed more than 100 compositions including "A Symphony of Some Humanity - Symphony #1 for Strings and Choir" and "All, In Joyful Song - A Carol In Three Movements."

In 2005, he founded the 501(c)3 nonprofit organization, the Humanity Project, and still serves as the group's president and primary program creator. Based in South Florida, the Humanity Project teaches respect for the unconditional equal value of every human being. Three core concepts form the foundation of every Humanity Project program: respect for all, the importance of diversity and the need for self-worth. www.thehumanityproject.com

Knotts is among fewer than 50,000 Americans whose biography is included in the Marquis "Who's Who In America" and "Who's Who in the World," the standard biographical references. In 2019, Marquis honored him with its Lifetime Achievement Award, given to fewer than 5 percent of all those listed in their 'Who's Who' volumes.

www.rsknotts.com